Rosa's Very Big Job

By
ELLEN MAYER

Illustrated by
SARAH VONTHRON-LAVER

STAR BRIGHT BOOKS
CAMBRIDGE MASSACHUSETTS

Published by Star Bright Books in 2016.

Text copyright © 2016 Ellen Mayer
Illustrations copyright © 2016 Star Bright Books

The name Star Bright Books and the Star Bright Books logo are registered
trademarks of Star Bright Books, Inc. The name Small Talk Books® is a
registered trademark of Star Bright Books and Ellen Mayer.
Please visit: www.starbrightbooks.com.
For bulk orders, please email: orders@starbrightbooks.com,
or call customer service at: (617) 354-1300.

Printed on paper from sustainable forests.

Hardcover ISBN-13: 978-1-59572-748-0
Paperback ISBN-13: 978-1-59572-749-7
Star Bright Books / MA / 00106160
Printed in China / TOPPAN / 9 8 7 6 5 4 3 2 1

Library of Congress Cataloging-in-Publication Data is available.

To Jenny, who loved to help –EM

To my lovely family near and far who have always believed in me!—SVL

Rosa was little, but she knew she could help.

She was too little to shop for groceries. That's what Mama was going to do.

She was too little to cook the dinner.
That's what Mama would do later
when she came home.

But maybe . . . she could help
with the laundry!

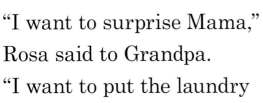

"I want to surprise Mama,"
Rosa said to Grandpa.
"I want to put the laundry
away. Please help me,
Grandpa!"

"That's a lot to do," answered
Grandpa. "Especially before
Mama gets home from
shopping."

"Come on, Grandpa! Get up,"
said Rosa.

"It's difficult to carry these
enormous piles," sighed Grandpa.

"Be careful,"
warned Rosa. "You
dropped the sheet."

"It's difficult to keep these clothes folded," complained Grandpa.

"Be neat," said Rosa.
"Like me."

"It's difficult to keep this jacket from sliding off the hanger," said Grandpa.

"Zip it up," explained Rosa. "Then it stays on."

"Wonderful work!" sighed Grandpa.
"You are terrific at doing laundry, Rosa.
And I am exhausted."

"Wait," said Rosa.
"We are not done yet."

"Come on, Grandpa! Get in the boat," cried Rosa. "Help me sail back to there."

"It's difficult to sail around this enormous rock!" said Grandpa.

"Be careful," warned Rosa.

"It's difficult to sail over this enormous wave!" said Grandpa.

"Don't tip over," warned Rosa.

"Watch out, there's a dangerous storm ahead!" shouted Grandpa. "I can't hold the sail in this strong wind."

"Hold tight," ordered Rosa.
"Use both hands."

"Phew," sighed Grandpa. "I'm glad that's over. That sure was a dangerous trip, Rosa."

"Wait," said Rosa.
"We are not done yet."

"Help me catch that enormous fish," said Rosa.

"You'll need a fishing rod to catch that fish," replied Grandpa.

"It's difficult to catch this fish!" cried Rosa.

"I'm home!" called Mama.

"Catch that fish!"
whispered Grandpa.
"I hear Mama at the door."

"Thank you, Grandpa!"
whispered back Rosa.

"Oh my," said Mama,
"Where is all the laundry?"

"SURPRISE, MAMA!" called Rosa. "We put all the laundry away. It was a very big job. We carried enormous piles. Grandpa dropped things. And I picked them up. It was very difficult for Grandpa. He got exhausted. But not me. I am terrific at laundry!"

"You are a terrific helper, Rosa," said Mama. "And a very big girl! Thank you so much for putting the laundry away."

"And there's another surprise, Mama,"
said Rosa. "It was very dangerous . . ."

". . . but we caught a fish for dinner!"

A Note for Parents, Grandparents and Caregivers

Just like Rosa in this story, young children love big words. And just as Grandpa does, adults can introduce big words when they talk with preschoolers. Grandpa uses some big words as he plays with little Rosa—*difficult, enormous, terrific, exhausted* and *dangerous*. He uses these big words in ways that are easy to understand, as the two of them have fun doing a chore, and then pretending together. Rosa is so proud when she learns to use these new big words herself!

The more you talk with young children, the faster their language grows. Your playful conversations help build the child's vocabulary, along with his or her memory, imagination, and self-confidence. A rich vocabulary and lots of experience with storytelling—in English or in a child's home language— make it easier to learn to read and to adjust to school.

You don't have to talk like a dictionary to build a preschooler's vocabulary! Just follow the child's lead, share your knowledge, and have fun!

—**Dr. Betty Bardige,** expert on young children's language and literacy development and author of the books *At a Loss for Words, Building Literacy with Love,* and *Talk to Me, Baby!*